Wideawake Mice in danger!

and other stories

Produced by Allegra Publishing Ltd, London
for Mercury Books Ltd
Editor : Felicia Law
Designer : Karen Radford

Published by
Mercury Junior an imprint of Mercury Books
20 Bloomsbury Street
London WC1B 3JH, UK

ISBN 978 1845600396

Wideawake Mice
in danger!

and other stories

Sheila McCullagh

Illustrated by
Prue Theobalds, Tony Morris, Gavin Rowe,
John Dillow, Bookmatrix, India

Mercury Junior

The Wideawake Mice were toy mice in
Mr Wideawake's toy shop.

One evening, the Magician came into the shop.
He didn't see the Wideawake Mice but he
accidentally spilt some magic dust all over them.

When the moon shone on them later that night,
the Wideawake Mice came alive. They crept
out of the shop through a hole under the door
and found themselves in the square. They made
their home in the market place, but this was
very dangerous. So they moved to the hole
in the tree, safe in the Magician's garden.

This story tells what happened next…

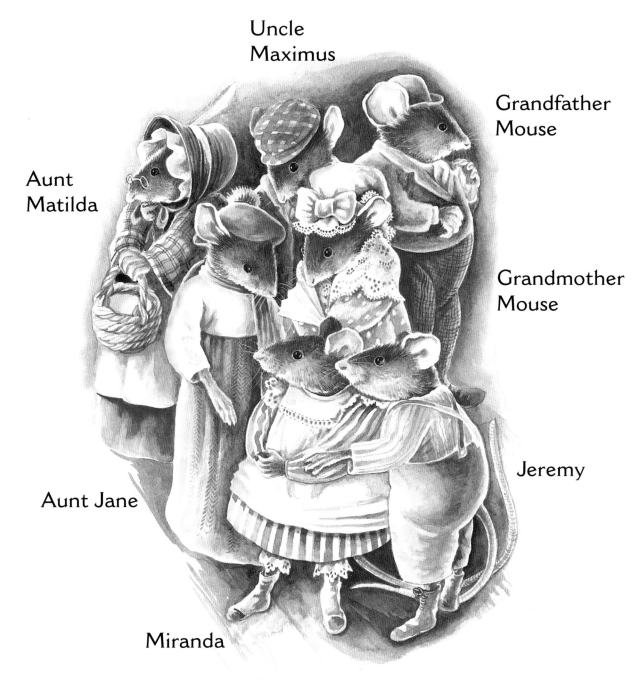

Uncle
Maximus

Grandfather
Mouse

Aunt
Matilda

Grandmother
Mouse

Aunt Jane

Jeremy

Miranda

5

The Wideawake Mice go to Market

Gita was a little girl who lived in Puddle Lane. One hot day, she tied a red handkerchief over her head and ran up the lane to the Magician's house. As she got to the gate that led into the garden, she saw a little mouse sitting on the wall in the sunshine. The little mouse (who was Aunt Jane) was wearing a long skirt, a blouse and a hat.

At that moment, a puff of wind blew Gita's handkerchief off. But Gita was so surprised to see the little mouse that she didn't notice. Aunt Jane disappeared over the wall. Gita ran back down the lane to tell her brother Hari.

But before she found Hari, Gita met Mrs Pitter-Patter.

"Oh, Mrs Pitter-Patter," cried Gita. "There's a mouse on the garden wall. And the mouse is wearing a skirt and a hat!"

"Don't tell such stories, Gita," said Mrs Pitter-Patter. "Mice don't wear hats." "This one does," said Gita.

"Gita, you mustn't tell stories!" said Mrs Pitter-Patter. She shook her finger at Gita, and went off up the lane. Gita went to find Hari.

Aunt Jane ran back to the big hole under the hollow tree. On her way, she saw Gita's red handkerchief, which the wind had blown into the garden.

She went down into the hole and found the other mice all talking together.

Uncle Maximus was talking louder
than any of the others.

"I'm hungry," said Uncle Maximus.
"I'm **VERY** hungry."
"We're all hungry,"
said Grandfather Mouse.

"It's market day tomorrow,"
said Chestnut. "I always go
to the market on market day."

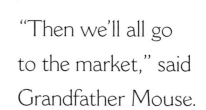

"Then we'll all go
to the market," said
Grandfather Mouse.

"We can't **ALL** go to market," said Chestnut. "Tom Cat will be there. Tom Cat is hungry too you know. If we all go to market, Tom Cat would be sure to catch one of us."

That made everyone shiver.

"I – I'm not very well," said Uncle Maximus. "I think I'll stay at home. You can bring something back for me to eat."

"I'll go to market tomorrow," said Chestnut. "Jeremy and Miranda can come with me. They can run the fastest. The rest of you had better stay at home. We'll bring food back with us."

Grandfather Mouse wanted to go too, but Chestnut said that he was much too slow, and Grandmother Mouse said that he had a cold.

Aunt Jane said nothing. She went back to
the garden. She found Gita's handkerchief
and pulled it into the hole.
Then she cut it up and
made four little red sacks.

"What are they for?"
asked Chestnut.
"To take to market,"
said Aunt Jane.
"But there are four of
them," said Chestnut.
"I'm going to market,
too," said Aunt Jane.

And she said it so firmly, that
Chestnut didn't say any more.

The next morning, before it was light,
the four little mice went down
Puddle Lane. Each little
mouse had a little
red sack.

They were all going
to market.

As they came to the end of Puddle Lane
they saw the big dog. He was fast asleep.

"Shh!" whispered Chestnut.
"Don't wake him."

They tip-toed past.
The dog's nose twitched.
He dreamt about mice,
but he didn't wake up.

It was just getting light
when they came to the
market building.

The four little mice ran up a post.
They hid in the roof and waited.
They hadn't long to wait.

Soon they heard people
in the market below.

The four little mice looked down.
The people were setting up tables.

There were bowls of nuts,
and big round cheeses.
There were cakes
and biscuits and
loaves of bread.

"I'm hungry,"
said Jeremy.
"I'm **VERY** hungry."

"Wait until the market is full of people,"
said Chestnut. "Then they won't see us.
They'll be too busy shopping."

As soon as the people came
into the market, the little mice
ran down the post. Nobody
noticed them.

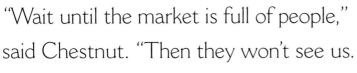

They ran about the
floor, looking for food.

18

They began to eat.
They ate cheese and nuts.
They ate cake and biscuits.
(People were very careless,
and dropped all kinds of
things on the floor.)

When they couldn't eat
any more, the four little
mice filled the red sacks
with food.

The sacks were soon full.

"We'll go home now," said Aunt Jane.

At that moment, Chestnut saw
Mrs Pitter-Patter. Mrs Pitter-Patter
had come to market and her
shopping basket was full. She
put down her basket while
she took out her purse to
pay for a cheese.

"Quick!" said Chestnut. "Hide in the basket. We'll get a ride home. That will be **MUCH** safer than running across the square."

As quickly as they could, all the mice picked up their sacks and hid in Mrs Pitter-Patter's basket. Mrs Pitter-Patter put away her purse. She picked up her basket and set off for Puddle Lane.

Mrs Pitter-Patter came to her house in Puddle Lane.
She put down her basket, and took out her key.

"Now we must run,"
said Chestnut.
"Wait until I see if it's safe,"
said Aunt Jane.

And she ran out on to
the handle of the basket.

Mrs Pitter-Patter bent down to pick
up her basket. She saw Aunt Jane
sitting on the handle.

"Help!" cried Mrs Pitter-Patter.
"Help! Help!"

She ran into the house.
She left the basket in
Puddle Lane.

Miranda and Jeremy, Aunt Jane
and Chestnut all scrambled out
and ran off up the lane.

23

There was a great feast that night
in the hole under the tree.

Aunt Jane and Chestnut,
Miranda and Jeremy were
so full that they couldn't
eat very much. But they
all had a wonderful time.

As for Mrs Pitter-Patter,
she never again told Gita
that she was telling stories.

Danger in
the Magician's
garden

It was a fine warm evening. The Wideawake Mice were all out in the Magician's garden. Uncle Maximus and Aunt Matilda were sitting on a tree root by the hollow tree, when Jeremy came home with a sack full of nuts.

"Where did you find these?" asked Uncle Maximus, helping himself to a nut. "On the steps of the Magician's house," said Jeremy. "There are lots more. Bits of cheese too, and cake crumbs."

"I think I'll go and see for myself,"
said Uncle Maximus. He climbed
down from the tree root.

"I'll come too," said Aunt Matilda.
"I'll just put this sack inside
and then I'll come and
show you the way,"
said Jeremy.

Jeremy left the sack in the big hole
under the hollow tree and then he
set off with Uncle Maximus and Aunt
Matilda towards the Magician's house.

28

Jeremy led the way through the grass, climbing
over rocks and running under bushes. Before they
had gone very far, Uncle Maximus was out of breath.

"Isn't there an easier way to go?"
he panted.
"Yes, there is," said Jeremy.
"But this is the safest way."

"Safest!" cried Uncle Maximus.
"Do you mean that it's
DANGEROUS out
here in the garden?"

"Well, you don't know
who might be about,"
said Jeremy.

"I'm going back," said Uncle Maximus.
"I don't feel very well."
"Don't you want any cake crumbs?"
asked Jeremy.
Uncle Maximus looked very
unhappy. "Of course I do,"
he said, rather crossly. "But I
can't get to the steps and back.
I'm not well. I can't do it."

"You go home, Maximus,"
said Aunt Matilda. "I'll go
on with Jeremy, and bring
some crumbs back for you."

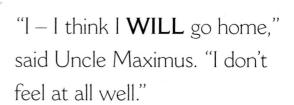

"I – I think I **WILL** go home,"
said Uncle Maximus. "I don't
feel at all well."

Uncle Maximus went back to the hollow tree
and Jeremy went on with Aunt Matilda.
Suddenly, a blackbird in a tree over
their heads began to scold.

Aunt Matilda stopped.
"What's that blackbird
saying?" she asked.

"I don't know," said Jeremy.
He sniffed the air. "Can you
smell anything?" he asked.

"There's a very strange smell,"
said Aunt Matilda. "I don't like it."
"Nor do I," said Jeremy.

At that moment, a big fox
jumped out from behind
a bush.

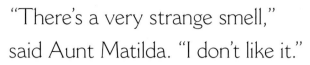

He seized Aunt Matilda in his
mouth. Jeremy leapt sideways,
behind some stones.

He peeped out between two of the stones
and saw the fox standing there, with Aunt
Matilda in his jaws.

Jeremy was very frightened
but he wasn't going to run
away if there was a chance
of saving Aunt Matilda.
He poked up his head
over a stone.

"Put her down!" he cried.
"You mustn't hurt anyone
in the Magician's garden.
The Magician said so."

The fox put Aunt Matilda down on the ground and held her there with his paw.

He was planning to eat Aunt Matilda for supper, but he thought that if only Jeremy would come a little nearer, he might have two mice for supper, not just one.

"The Magician said nothing to me," he said. "I don't live in his garden. I live in the wood."

"I don't care where you live," said Jeremy.
"I'll tell the Magician. When the Magician
finds out that you've hurt Aunt Matilda
you'll be sorry!"

"I'm a little deaf," said the fox.
"I can't hear what you say.
Come nearer."

Two heads appeared over the bushes.
Hari and Gita had been playing ball
in the Magician's garden.

They were going home,
when they heard a noise,
and they stopped to see
what it was.

As they looked, the fox made
a sudden leap towards Jeremy.

36

Hari still had the ball in his hand. As quick
as a flash, he threw it straight at the fox.
"Get off!" he cried. "Get away!"

The ball hit the fox in mid-air.
It didn't hurt him but it startled him.

Jeremy ducked down
behind some stones.

The fox dropped to the ground. He saw Hari
and Gita, and ran off under the bushes. Hari
and Gita chased after him.

Jeremy came out from behind
the stones, and ran to Aunt Matilda.
She was struggling to her feet.
Her dress was all torn and muddy
and she could scarcely stand.

"Are you hurt?" cried Jeremy.

Aunt Matilda shook her
head. She couldn't speak.

Jeremy helped her to limp
across to the stones.

"Wait here for a bit," he said.
"You'll be quite safe here.
Look – there's a little hole
under this stone. We can
hide in that."

They crept under the
stone and waited.

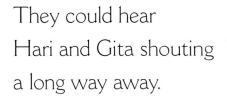

They could hear
Hari and Gita shouting
a long way away.

The shouting stopped. Jeremy came
out of the hole. The blackbird had
stopped scolding and was down
on the ground, looking for worms.

Jeremy sniffed the air.
The fox had gone.

Jeremy went back to Aunt Matilda.

"It's safe to go home now," he said.
"I don't know if I can," whispered
poor Aunt Matilda. "I'm almost
too frightened to move."

"We must go while it's safe,"
said Jeremy. "I'll go first."

He crept out of the hole
and Aunt Matilda limped
after him.

41

A few minutes later, the two little mice crept safely back down the mousehole and under the hollow tree.
The other mice were all there.
They had heard Hari and Gita shouting and had run home as fast as they could.
"I'll never go into the garden again," said Uncle Maximus, when he heard what had happened.
"Someone will have to go," said Aunt Jane. "We have to go out to find food. But we'll be very careful."

"You have to be careful all the time, when you're a real wood mouse." said Chestnut.

Hari and Gita came back through the garden
looking for the mice. But the mice had gone.

"They must be all right," said Hari.
"They must have gone home."
"We must tell the Magician
about that fox," said Gita.
"Yes, we must," said Hari.
"It's not safe for the mice,
with a fox in the garden."

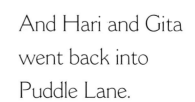

And Hari and Gita
went back into
Puddle Lane.

Jeremy's Ride

It was Friday evening, and the Wideawake Mice were in Candletown market.

"It's getting dark," said Grandfather Mouse.
"We must go home."
"Let me finish this nut," said Jeremy.
"You start off and we'll follow," said Chestnut.
He had just found another nut too,
and he didn't want to leave it.
"Well don't be long," said Grandfather Mouse,
setting off across the square.

"We can run much faster than
Uncle Maximus," said Jeremy.
"Yes, but we mustn't be long,"
said Chestnut. "Tom Cat
comes out in the evening."
Jeremy finished his nut.
"All right," he said, "Let's go."

45

They had almost reached the entrance to Puddle Lane
when Chestnut stopped. His whiskers twitched.
"There's someone about,"
he said.

Tom Cat sprang out of
the shadows, and leapt
towards them.

"Run!" cried Chestnut,
rushing off to one side.
"Run for your life!"

Jeremy raced towards Puddle Lane. Tom Cat stopped for a second. He wasn't sure which mouse to follow. Then he sprang after Jeremy.

The second's pause had given Jeremy just time to reach the archway that led to Puddle Lane.

If he had tried to run through it, Tom Cat would have caught him. But he didn't. He ran up the wall of the archway as fast as he could.

Tom Cat leapt up after him, but Jeremy
was just out of reach. Tom Cat fell back
to the ground. Jeremy scrambled
up the old wall, clinging to
the cracks between the
stones, until he came
to the windowsill.

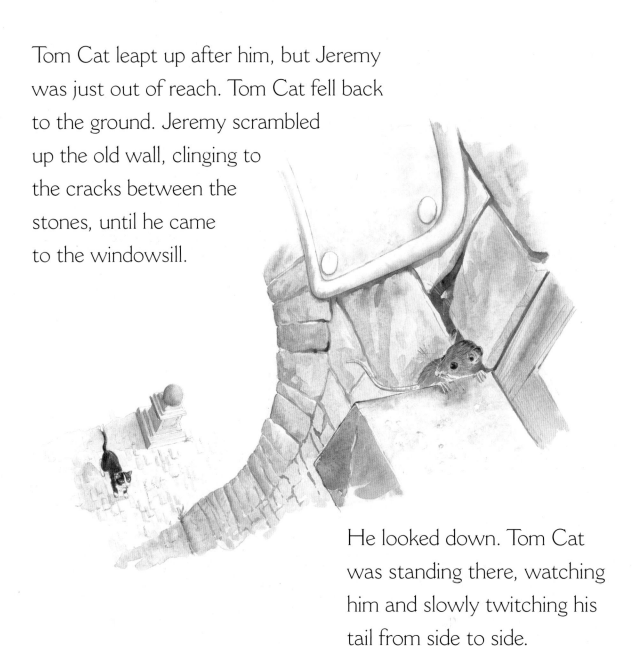

He looked down. Tom Cat
was standing there, watching
him and slowly twitching his
tail from side to side.

"That was a near thing," said a squeaky little voice in his ear. Jeremy jumped round, and saw a little mouse looking out of a hole between two stones.

"You'd better come inside," said the mouse. "I know Tom Cat. He'll just sit there and wait for you."

Jeremy looked down. Tom Cat was sitting on the stones below, looking up.

Jeremy shivered, and followed the mouse through the hole. He found himself in the room over the archway leading to Puddle Lane. The room was empty and there were cobwebs on the windows.

"I'm Whiskers," said the mouse, as soon as Jeremy was safely inside. "I live here."
"I thought mice were called after the names of trees," said Jeremy.
"Wood mice have names like that," said Whiskers.
"I'm a house mouse. I have a proper mouse name and a proper house to live in. I don't live outside in the rain."

"I live in the Magician's garden," said Jeremy, "and I've got to get home."

"I should stay here till morning, if I were you," said Whiskers. "If you go now, Tom Cat will be waiting for you."

"But if I'm not home soon, Grandfather will come to look for me," said Jeremy. "And Tom Cat will see him. Grandfather would never get away from Tom Cat. He can't run fast enough."

Whiskers ran up the wall on the far side of the room and looked out of another window up Puddle Lane.

"Just come and have a look," he said.
Jeremy ran across the room, and
climbed up beside him.

"What did I tell you?" said
Whiskers. "Tom Cat's
there waiting."

Jeremy looked down. Tom Cat had
come through the archway and was
watching him from inside Puddle Lane.

"But I've got to get home,"
said Jeremy.
"There's one way you might
manage it," said Whiskers.
"That is, if you're not too
frightened."
"What's that?" asked Jeremy.

"I saw the Magician go into
the square a little while ago,"
said Whiskers.

"He'll come home this way
soon. You could jump down on
his hat as he comes through the
archway and get a ride home.
He'd never notice you."

"I'll try," said Jeremy.
"You've got to do more than just try," said Whiskers. "If you miss, you'll land on the ground and Tom Cat will get you."

Jeremy shivered. "I — I think I can do it," he said. "Grandfather will be coming soon."

"This way then," said Whiskers. He led the way to a little hole between two stones.

The two mice crept through the hole and out on to the windowsill. The moon was shining down and Jeremy could see Tom Cat, watching them from the stones below.

"Listen!" said Whiskers.
"Here's the Magician."

Jeremy heard slow footsteps
coming over the stones. He felt
almost too frightened to move.
He looked down and saw the
Magician's flat hat below him.

"Now!" squeaked Whiskers. "Jump!" Jeremy jumped.
He felt himself falling through the air and for one
dreadful moment, he thought that he had missed.

Then his feet landed
on the Magician's hat
and he held on with all his claws.

His heart was beating so loudly that it
sounded like a drum banging in his ears.

56

When he had recovered a little, he looked around him.
He was being carried down Puddle Lane at a steady
pace on the Magician's head. He looked back. The lights
in the houses shone through the windows
and he could see quite well.

Tom Cat was creeping after
them, in the shadows at the
side of the lane.

Jeremy wasn't cold but
he found himself shivering.
They came to the gates
of the Magician's garden.
As the Magician turned
to shut the gate, he saw
Tom Cat.

"Shoo! Scat! Be off with you!"
cried the Magician.
Tom Cat stopped. "Scat!"
cried the Magician again.

He snapped his fingers.
A little ball of fire fell into the
lane just in front of Tom Cat.

Tom Cat turned and
fled. He ran back down
the lane as fast as he
could run, with the
little ball of fire
chasing after him.

The Magician laughed
and snapped his fingers again.
The ball of fire disappeared. Jeremy didn't wait.
As quick as a flash he jumped on to the gate
and ran down the gate to the garden.

As he got to the hollow tree, he met Grandfather Mouse.

"Jeremy!" cried Grandfather. "I'm so glad to see you.
Chestnut came home without you. He came home
the back way. I was just coming
to see where you were."

"I'm so glad to be home,"
said Jeremy, still shivering.
"I've had such an adventure."

"Come inside and tell us all
about it," said Grandfather.
"You're quite safe now."

And he followed Jeremy into
the hole under the hollow tree.

A Present
for Aunt Matilda

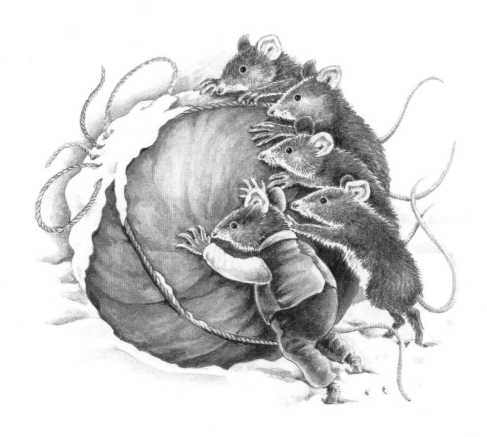

It was winter in Puddle Lane. Everything was covered in snow. The Wideawake Mice, who lived under the hollow tree in the Magician's garden, were very hungry.

The birds had eaten all the berries, and the seeds in the garden were under the snow.

"It's market day today," said Chestnut.
"I'll go to the market and get some food."

"We'll go with you,"
said Jeremy and Miranda.
"So will I," said Aunt Jane.
"You'll have to run on all
four feet," said Chestnut,
"or you'll sink in the
snow. You can't do
that in a skirt."

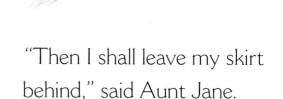

"Then I shall leave my skirt
behind," said Aunt Jane.

"I'm going too," said Grandfather Mouse.
"I can run very well on four feet if I take
off my coat."
"What about us?" asked Uncle Maximus.
"We'll bring some food back for you,"
said Grandfather Mouse.

The five little
mice went out.
They set off
across the snow

They were half way down Puddle Lane when
they saw Miss Baker. She was carrying a parcel.
"Hide!" squeaked Chestnut.

The mice all hid in the snow beside the
stone steps leading to Miss Baker's
front door.

Miss Baker stopped at the door of
Miss Match's house. Miss Match
and Miss Matilda Match
were very old ladies.
They were Miss
Baker's aunts.

Miss Matilda Match loved cheese.
Miss Baker had been to the market and
bought her a big round Dutch cheese.

Miss Baker knocked on Miss Match's door.
There was no answer. "They must be out,"
she said.

She put the cheese
down on the top step.
She took out a piece
of paper and wrote
'Aunt Matilda' on it.
She tucked the paper
under the string on
top of the parcel.
Then she went on
up the lane into
her own house.

Aunt
Matilda

As soon as Miss Baker was safely indoors the Wideawake Mice came out. They ran on down the lane.

But as they passed Miss Match's door, they smelt the smell of cheese.

Chestnut ran up the steps and the others all followed him.

"There's cheese in this parcel," said Chestnut.
"Let's make a hole in it and see."
"Wait a minute," said Grandfather Mouse.

Chestnut had knocked Miss Baker's
paper off the top of the parcel.
Grandfather Mouse looked at it.

"This says 'Aunt Matilda'," he said,
in a very surprised tone. "It must
be a present for Aunt Matilda.
I wonder why it was left here."

"Let's take it home to Aunt Matilda,"
said Aunt Jane. "We can all eat it."

"Come back here," said Grandfather
Mouse, climbing the steps and going
behind the cheese.
"Now - push! Push hard!"

The cheese rolled down
the steps into the snow.

The mice ran down after it
and began to push the cheese.
The cheese rolled slowly up
Puddle Lane.

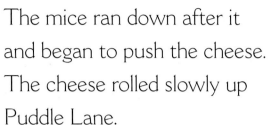

It was very heavy, and by the time
they got to Mr Puffle's house they
were tired out.

"It's no good," said Aunt Jane. "We'll never get it home like this. It's too heavy. Let's make a hole in the paper and eat some of the cheese. We shall feel much stronger when we've had something to eat."

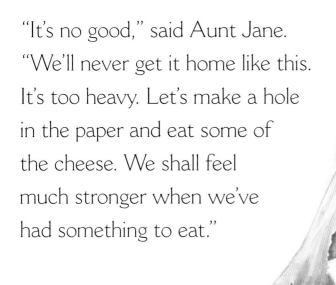

Chestnut and Jeremy tore a hole in the paper and the mice began to eat. They were very hungry and it wasn't long before they had eaten a big hole into the middle of the cheese.

The mice were so busy eating that they didn't hear
Sarah and Gita coming along the lane in the snow.
"What's that?" said Sarah, as she saw the cheese.
She picked it up.

The little mice squeaked
with fright. Sarah dropped
the cheese.

The mice fell out and ran
off up Puddle Lane as fast
as they could run.

Sarah picked the cheese up again.
"Someone must have bought
this in the market," she said.
"But it's no good now."

"The mice must be very
hungry in all this snow,"
said Gita.

"Let's take it to the hollow tree in the Magician's
garden," said Sarah. "That's where the mice live.
I've seen them there. Let's take it for them."

Grandfather Mouse, Aunt Jane,
Chestnut, Jeremy and Miranda
ran back into the hole under the
hollow tree, tumbling over each
other as they ran.

"Whatever's the matter?"
asked Grandmother Mouse.

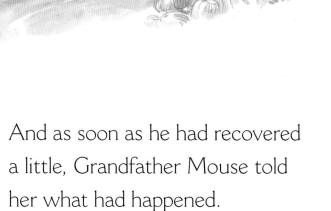

And as soon as he had recovered
a little, Grandfather Mouse told
her what had happened.

"You've all had some cheese, but I'm **SO** hungry," said Uncle Maximus. "I don't think I shall live very much longer if I don't have something to eat."

"We'll go out again," said Grandfather Mouse. "We'll find something for you."

Chestnut lifted his nose. His whiskers twitched. "Cheese!" cried Chestnut. "I can smell cheese."

He ran back up the hole to the hollow tree. There, by the hollow tree, was the big round red Dutch cheese.

"Cheese!" cried Chestnut again. "The cheese is here!"

All the other mice came running up into the hollow tree.

When the moon shone down into the
hollow tree that night, there was no
sign of the big Dutch cheese. All that
was left of it was piled up, in little
bits, in the big hole under the
tree. The Wideawake Mice
were all feeling very full
and very comfortable.

"It was a wonderful present,"
said Aunt Matilda, sleepily.
"I wonder who sent it to me?"

Nobody answered.
The Wideawake Mice
were all asleep.

The Fox and
the Magician

The Wideawake Mice were all in the big hole under the hollow tree, when Chestnut came down the mousehole from the garden.

"It's time we went out to look for food," he said.

"I don't think I can go out this evening," said Aunt Matilda.
"Nor can I," said Uncle Maximus.

Uncle Maximus didn't want to go because he was feeling frightened, but Aunt Matilda really wasn't very well.

Aunt Matilda had nearly been eaten by a fox the evening before. She had escaped, but she was still feeling very shaken. She was very upset too because her dress was all torn and muddy.

All the other mice were growing more like wood mice every day. But Aunt Matilda couldn't forget that she was a Wideawake Mouse. She liked to look pretty and neat, and when she looked at her torn dress she felt very unhappy.

The sun was beginning to set. There were long
shadows in the garden as the Wideawake
Mice came out of the hole and scattered
to look for food. Chestnut went off
to find a hole that he had
dug the day before.

Aunt Jane went with
Grandfather and Grandmother
Mouse to look for nuts on the
steps of the Magician's house.

And Jeremy and Miranda went off
to a bush of berries near the wall.

They found the bush without any trouble
and climbed up to eat the berries.
They had each eaten three and
were beginning to think that
a few nuts would be very
pleasant, when Miranda
suddenly said,

"Look Jeremy!
What's that?"

They looked down and saw a little doll lying in the long grass below them. Miranda and Jeremy didn't know it, but the doll belonged to Gita.

Gita and Sarah had been playing in the garden that afternoon and Gita had dropped the doll as they were going back to the gate.

Jeremy and Miranda ran down to the
ground to take a closer look.
"It's like the dolls we used to
see in Mr Wideawake's toy shop,"
said Jeremy.
"It isn't alive like us, is it?" asked
Miranda.
"Of course it isn't," said Jeremy.
"We only came alive when the
Magician spilt magic dust all
over us."

"It's got a lovely dress," said Miranda. "Let's take it
back to Aunt Matilda. It's just the right size.
A new dress would make her happy again."
"All right," said Jeremy.

They began to pull the doll home towards the
hollow tree. They had not gone far when
they came to some thick bushes.
The two little mice stopped.

"We shall spoil the dress if we
pull the doll through those," said
Miranda. "Let's take the dress off
and leave the doll here."

The long grass near the bushes stirred. Jeremy
and Miranda were so excited and so busy with
the doll that they forgot to look and listen.

The grass parted a little.
A long nose sniffed the air
and two bright eyes looked out.
It was the fox.

Very quietly, the fox moved forward, bit by bit.
Jeremy and Miranda still didn't see the fox
and the fox didn't make a sound.

He stood there
watching. Then he
stiffened, ready to pounce.

There was a sudden flash, and a noise
like a thunderclap. A ball of fire
burst over their heads.
The two little mice
leapt to one side
and hid under
a big stone.

The fox jumped back.

The Magician was standing by the bushes.
He looked straight at the fox.

"I hear that you have been hunting in my
garden," he said. "I have made a rule
and you must obey it. You can hunt
in the woods or in the fields but
not in my garden. If you hurt any
animals who live in my garden,
I shall turn you to stone."

The fox looked at the Magician
for a few moments. Then, without
a word, he turned and ran off.

Jeremy peeped out from under the stone. His whiskers twitched.

"There's no one here," he whispered. He crept out and Miranda followed him.

"Are you quite sure the fox has gone?" asked Miranda, looking all around.

"Didn't you hear what the Magician said?" asked Jeremy. "We're safe now."

"We must still be very careful.
Let's go home," said Miranda.

She picked up the dress and Jeremy
picked up the doll's hat. They set off
for the hollow tree.

When Aunt Matilda heard what the Magician
had said to the fox, she was so thankful
that she began to feel better at once.
And when she saw the dress and
hat that Jeremy and Miranda
had brought back for her,
she was so delighted that
she almost danced over
the tree roots.

She put on the dress at once, and
by the time she had had some
supper, she was her old self again.

94

Before the sun had quite
gone down, Gita and Sarah
came back to the garden to look
for Gita's doll. It was Sarah who
found it.

"Look Gita," cried Sarah picking
it up. "Here it is. But someone has taken
the doll's dress! Who could have done that?"

"I don't know, but I think I can guess," said Gita.
"I once saw a mouse on the garden wall. She was
dressed in a skirt. The mice who live in this garden
aren't like other mice. But I don't mind a bit.
Let's go home."

You can read more stories about the Wideawake Mice
in:
Stories of the Wideawake Mice

But the Wideawake Mice are not the only characters
who live in Puddle Lane. Mr Gotobed lives there and so does
Mrs Pitter-Patter and lots of other grown-ups. Then there are
the children, Hari and Gita and Davey and Sarah.
But by far the most important inhabitant of Puddle Lane
is the Magician. After all, his magic turns
everyone's lives upside down!
Read all about the magical adventures
of the people who live in the lane
in:
The Magician of Puddle Lane